Finn's Tale

J. A. Sandilands

Published in 2010 by Julie Sandilands

To purchase a copy of this book please visit:
www.juliesandilands.com
email:jules.sandilands@btinternet.com

Cover design / illustrations by Alexandra Jones
www.alexandrajones.co.uk

Foreword

This story is dedicated with much love to Duncan, who has always been encouraged to open his heart and mind to the world around him.

I would also like to acknowledge and thank all those who have been involved in the process of getting this book ready for print and distribution. A special thank you goes to Duncan for the hand drawn map on page four, and for his ideas and enthusiasm, which have been invaluable in the creation of this story.

'Aspire to your dreams – unto yourself be true'

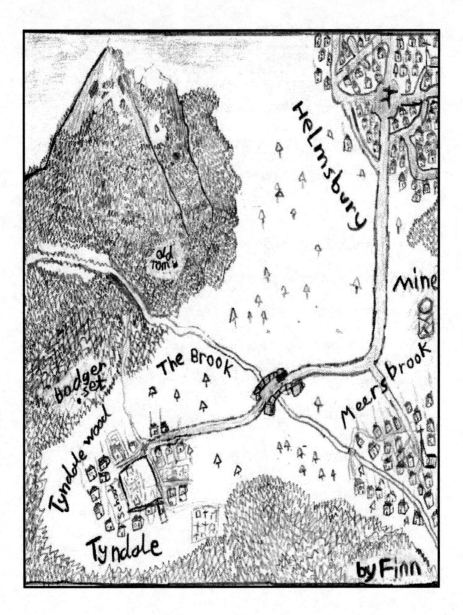

Chapter One

An Autumn Day

Golden autumn leaves fluttered down from the trees and the east wind blew through the branches. The air had a nip in it, reminding people that winter was on the way. For now, though, it was a mid-October afternoon at Tyndale Village School. Finn, as usual, was staring out of the window wishing he was kicking up the leaves in the woods rather than sitting at the wooden desk reciting numbers, which then made even more numbers.

"What's the use of this?" he thought to himself. "When am I ever going to use this? Imagine being in a life or death situation. What am I going to do? Recite times tables? Will that save my life?"

This wasn't an unusual state of mind for Finn. He was a twelve-year-old inquisitive boy who understood much about the workings and patterns of nature, the habits of the creatures that roamed around the village and the woods both by day and night. As each season unfolded, Finn never ceased to appreciate its individual wonder and purpose in the cycle of life. Schoolwork, however, was not and would not, seem important to him in the foreseeable future.

Finn was small in stature compared to other boys the same age, but strong. He could out-run any of his classmates in a race. His hair was a mousy brown, with a slight hint of ginger that became more apparent under the bright summer sun. He had vivid blue eyes, a small brown birthmark on his left cheek, and an abundance of freckles that covered his face throughout the summer. Finn's second-hand and homemade clothes were the object of teasing from other children as he grew up, but approval from his peers was not necessary in Finn's world and he was oblivious to their constant taunts.

Ten to three and the last bell rang, indicating the end of the school day. Within minutes he was climbing through the bracken and brambles up the slope to Tyndale Wood. He had a favourite place there where no one ever disturbed him. It was called Badgers Hollow and it was a shallow dip about half a mile from the edge of the wood. Finn sat down on the leaves, still wet from a midday shower. He closed his eyes and leant against the trunk of an oak tree. Now he felt at home. This is where he could let his mind relax yet focus on his surroundings, where thoughts about school and other problems were extinguished leaving him free to feel the peace and tranquillity of the moment. He knew every tree, bush, and pathway around Tyndale Wood and often thought he recognised the birds that would sit at a distance on a branch, looking at him and occasionally burst into song.

Finn was a friendly child and got on reasonably well with his peers, but his reluctance to join in with the games played in the playground, often left him isolated. Football and similar pursuits taken up by the other boys in the village just did not appeal to him as much as sitting in his space in the woods watching this part of the world go by. He would often dig his fingers into the soft wet soil and look for anything that moved. His favourite creatures to examine were the beetles and millipedes. He would examine each body part before tenderly placing the creature back into the ground.

This Friday afternoon was no different from any other. Every day Finn would revel in his release from the confines of the classroom and climb up to this sacred place before going home to start his chores. His mother had brought him up alone since his father had died when Finn was five years old. Finn didn't completely understand why his father had died, but he remembered he had coughed a lot, especially during the night. He supposed it had something to do with working down the mine in the next village. He knew that in his mother's eyes Finn's destiny was to work in that mine too. He closed his eyes and shuddered at the very thought of being trapped underground with no fresh air and no bird song. He remembered a school trip where the children had been taken by bus to see the mine firsthand and the conditions in which the men worked. It was regarded in the village as an honourable and respectable job and this had become embedded in village culture over the mine's hundred years' of existence. He remembered the stale smell as he stood at the top of the mineshaft and watched the men coming up from the coalface, exhausted and as black as the coal they had been digging. He had decided there and then that his future would have nothing to do with the mine at all.

He had seen his mother change over the years since his father's death. She rarely smiled any more and stooped as she walked, preferring to look down at the ground instead of straight ahead. Her hair had greyed prematurely and her hands often shook when she held her morning cup of tea. After his father's death two men in black suits had knocked on the door. Finn had tried to listen to the conversation from his bedroom.

"You will receive the normal pension, Mrs. O'Connor, which everyone gets in these circumstances. I'm afraid that's the best we can do. As you have already been told, there isn't any solid evidence that your husband's death was caused by working in the mine."

That normal pension was only a third of the weekly income that his father had brought into the house. His mother had sat on the chair after they had left, her head cradled in her hands. He had tried to comfort her, putting his small hand on her knee, but grief and despair held her head firmly in place and she did not look up. The family photograph in his mother's bedroom was the only real reminder of his father Finn had left. His memories of him became more and more distant as the years passed by.

He suddenly thought of his chores again. Feed the chickens, put them away, bring in logs for the fire, and sweep the back yard. His mind was peacefully going through what he had to do when suddenly and without any warning the tree bark gave way and Finn found himself tumbling down a dark, cylindrical tunnel. He landed with a thud against something hard. It was dark and all he could do was fumble over the surface with his hands to see if it would move. Move it did, but not by him. The wooden door (for it was a door, a back door) opened and Finn once again tumbled very ungraciously onto a cold stone floor. He blinked as the light from an oil lamp in the room temporarily blinded him after the darkness of the tunnel.

"'Going to stay there all day are you?" said a gruff voice directly above him.

As his vision returned he saw a badger's head with piecing black eyes staring down at him. The badger was standing on his hind legs which gave him the appearance of being quite tall. Apologising, Finn shuffled to his feet and looked about him.

"You can sit over here," said the badger pointing to a comfortable but shabby looking armchair by the fire.

"Knew you were going visit us," he said scratching his head, "but couldn't you use the front door like everyone else?"

"I'm sorry," spluttered Finn, "I'm not sure where your front door is."

They stared at each other for a few seconds when a noise at the far end of the room distracted them both. Another badger came into the room muttering under its breath.

"And I told you Arnold, to clear away those damn leaves by the door. And did you? No, like it's too much trouble."

She turned as she spoke and the last word out of her mouth trailed away into silence. She stared briefly at Finn and then at her husband.

"See I were right Amelia, he has come to visit, just like I said he would."

Amelia looked at Finn with a hint of suspicion in her eyes. "Well I'll put the kettle on shall I?" she said, breaking the awkward silence.

Finn sat in the armchair by the fire and looked around the small room. The walls were made of earth but covered with shelves on which ornaments and photo

13

frames stood. The earth ceilings were quite low and brushed the top of Arnold's head as he stood bolt upright in front of Finn. There was a wooden dining table and two rickety chairs at either side. A log fire burnt in a charcoaled hearth and a kettle sat neatly on a hook above it, steam gently blowing out of its lid.

It was Arnold who spoke next. "We know why you're here like. It don't take a genius to work it out. Not that we're not grateful that is, and we think it's a good idea, like, that you're going to help us."

The shock of finding himself not only in this room, but listening to badgers speaking to him did not seem to register as strange at all to his two hosts, as if this had happened many times before. After a few moments Finn found the courage to speak.

"I never meant to disturb you. I was just sitting there minding me own business. I'm sorry I broke your door and I think I should be getting back cause me ma will start to worry if I'm not back soon."

"Will you use the front door then, lad?" said Arnold pointing to the door that Amelia had just come through. "That one you came through, that's our emergency exit like."

Finn looked at both badgers, nodded his head and side-stepped gingerly out of the door. After he heard the door click behind him, he scrambled up a short tunnel and found himself not far from the tree he had been leaning against. He ran back down the hill and as he did he saw a shadow in the corner of his eye move quickly out of sight. He stopped momentarily, but the shadow had gone. Finn thought it must have been Old Tom whom he had often seen wandering around the woods.

He arrived home only a few minutes later than usual and his mother had not been disturbed by this fact as it happened on a regular basis. She continued to sit in her armchair directly in front of the fire, crocheting tablemats which brought much needed money into the household. They lived in a small stone thatched cottage that consisted of one living room, which also housed the kitchen, a small bathroom and two bedrooms. The house was sparsely furnished like most of the houses in the village. People were poor, but they appreciated what they had and did not waste time wishing for things that were financially out of their reach. A fire burned constantly in the hearth from the beginning of October until the end of May. The cottage was on one level so the rooms warmed up if the doors were left open. Finn's bedroom was the smaller of the two and had a wooden bed underneath the window. There was a small chest of drawers and one tall cupboard. Both were practically empty as Finn had very little in the way of toys or clothes.

Still shaken from his experience, Finn carried out his daily chores without giving much thought to what he was actually doing. He decided that evening as he sat with his mother before going to bed that it would not be a good idea to tell her what had happened. In fact he made the decision not to tell anyone what had happened. Later that night he lay in his bed trying to make sense of the day's events. He thought about Tom and whether or not Tom had seen him coming out of the badger's front door.

Old Tom lived in a small wooden shack in the middle of the wood. Some years before he had been a foreman down the mine and was well respected in the village. One winter, his wife and baby son both died after an acute dose of the flu and Tom's enthusiasm for life had left him on the same day. He returned to the mine shortly after and through a lack of concentration, his hand was trapped between two of the rail cars. He lost the forefinger and little finger on his left hand. The managers at the mine decided he was too much of a liability, paid him off and reminded him that the cottage belonged to the mine and they expected the keys back at the end of the week. Since then Tom had lived in the shack in the woods, keeping out of town during the day. His shabby appearance frightened the children, and mothers and fathers alike could be seen dragging them back in doors if he walked down the road.

Finn tried to forget about Tom, and about Arnold. He screwed his eyes shut hoping it would help him to drop off. He eventually fell asleep as the clock struck midnight.

Chapter Two

Proud Sycamores

The next day was a Saturday, which meant an hour longer than usual in bed. Any longer, though, and his mother would be hammering on his door, reminding him that the chickens were not capable of unlocking the hen hut from the inside, and putting their eggs on the kitchen table. Finn finished his chores and went out of the garden and up the lane as he usually did on a Saturday morning. The lane was lined on either side with a combination of oak and elm trees, which provided a welcome relief from the sun for walkers in the summer, and an arch of colour in the autumn.

He walked through the village, past the other cottages and watched the villagers bustle about as gardens got tended, yards got swept, and windows were cleaned. It was a small village with approximately three hundred residents. It consisted of a post office, which also served as a shop, an inn called the Stag, and the blacksmiths at the far end of the village. A bus passed through the village twice a day, and thrice on a Saturday, when it was full of shoppers hoping to find bargains in Helmsbury, the next main town eight miles away.

Crime was minimal and Albert Shutterswaite served as both the postmaster and the community policeman. As far as Finn knew, the only crime Albert had ever had to solve was the theft of two chickens from Mrs. Aylesbury's coop. She had accused Jack, a teenager who was still struggling to read and would put his head down when spoken to. Although Jack had never denied the accusation, it was later established, after a thorough investigation and a stake-out by PC Shutterswaite, that the culprit was in fact a female fox who had recently given birth to three cubs. No apology was ever offered to Jack by Mrs. Aylesbury who had continued to tarnish his reputation in the village shop.

Life was quiet in Tyndale and nobody ever complained they wanted it any other way.

As Finn walked out of the village and towards the woods, he was hit by something hard on the back of his head. He turned, holding his hand against the bump on his scalp and saw three boys walking up the road behind him. The tallest of the boys picked up another conker and threw it at him. This time Finn ducked and it missed, whistling past his ear. He recognised the boy from school. His name was Christian and he was the eldest son of Mr Jones, one of the top managers at the mine. Christian was the school bully and used his father's position to intimidate the other children whose fathers worked down the mine in more menial positions.

Christian was the most spoilt child in Tyndale. No matter what new toy came into the shops, it wasn't long before Christian was proudly showing it off at school or on the village green. It also wasn't long before it was broken or discarded ready for next piece of fashion to land on his lap. The Jones' family were the first in the village to possess a black and white TV, much to Christian's delight as he recalled the programmes he had watched, to the other children, who listened, amazed at the fact that moving pictures with sound could come out of a small wooden box.

Every spring Christian would have a birthday party and all the children in the village (apart from Finn and

Jack), were invited. The children would talk for days about the magnificent time they had had. No expense was spared, with clowns and magicians hired to keep the children entertained. On the same evening, the parents would gather and another party would follow. Finn would hear the music and laughter as he sat in the oak tree by the garden gate. A few years ago he had felt hurt at being so publically snubbed. Now, it was a relief and Finn had no desire whatsoever to see inside the huge house.

Christian particularly disliked Finn, and took every opportunity to call him names or inflict physical injury. Finn's tactic had always been to stay out of Christian's way, but that wasn't going to be an option this morning.

"Oi, Tink," shouted Christian.

Tink was a nickname for the travelling people who occasionally visited the village and sold their trinkets or read palms. They were looked down upon by most of the villagers who blamed them for anything that went missing whilst they were around. Finn, however, had found them fascinating and looked forward to their annual visit. He had been drawn to their camp in the dusk light, the music and laughter, the flickering fires fuelling his curiosity. The gypsies had welcomed Finn into their gathering and he had sat around the fire as one of them, listening to the tales being told by the older men in the group. He had befriended one of the gypsy boys called Ryan and they had roamed the woods together. Finn had finally found somebody who knew about nature and enjoyed the outdoors as much he did. Because of this association, Finn soon acquired the nickname of 'Tink' by the other children, and some of their parents who looked on disapprovingly, keeping their own children away.

Christian walked up to Finn and put his face close to his. "Got any money?" he growled.

"I don't have any money, you know that."

"Yeah, we know that, don't we boys?" Christian scoffed. "We heard that your ma aint got no money either and that you eat pig swill."

All three boys howled with laughter. Finn took a step back to make his escape but before he could turn he felt the impact of a fist on his face and fell to the ground. He looked up as the boys ran back down the lane and into the village. His eyes stung with tears from the blow, and also the remark about his mother, who he knew was doing her best to provide for him. Using his sleeve, he wiped away the blood from his nose, hauled himself back to his feet and continued up the lane.

Finn reached the edge of the woods and hesitated. Should he go back to where he was yesterday, or should he avoid that area completely and head towards the west side of the wood? After a moment or two, he decided to head westward and explore the part of the woods where three tall sycamore trees proudly stood. As he walked, the leaves crunched under his feet, there had been a light frost during the night. The sunlight channelled its way through the trees, through the last few remaining leaves desperately clinging to the branches. The air was clean and crisp and Finn breathed deeply so he could watch his breath being exhaled into the cold air. Nothing seemed untoward or unnatural today and the birds and squirrels were going about their daily business as usual. He watched the squirrels as they scampered up the tree bark, jumping from branch to branch embarking on a game of chase.

Finn made his way towards the ridge where the sycamores were. It was quite steep and very slippery, with patches of ground still frozen because they were shielded from the sun by the trees. He took three large steps and on the third step stood on something sharp. He let out a yell. The pain in his foot was excruciating and he fell backwards down the ridge. Thinking he had sliced off half his foot, he pulled off his boot and sock and looked to see what was sticking out of the sole of his foot. What he saw could only be described as a large clear glass pin. Before he could pull it out a high-pitched voice rang in his ears.

"There it is. You've got it. No you've stolen it. It's not yours and I want it back. Give it to me now I say, give it to me."

Standing in front of him was the strangest looking man he had ever seen. The man was short in stature, about three feet tall. He had a mass of jet-black curly hair, a round ruddy face, and he was dressed in a gold and green tunic with a black belt clipped around a large tummy. He scowled at Finn and, without a hint of what he was going to do, the man leapt forward and without any care pulled the clear pin out of Finn's foot. Finn yelled in pain. He looked up, tears clouding his vision, but the man had disappeared in an instant. Finn looked at his foot to assess the damage but it showed no sign of injury and the pain had disappeared as soon as the pin had been removed.

As he started to stand up a familiar voice came from behind one of the sycamore trees.

"'Having quite a week, aren't you?" Arnold the badger moved into the sunlight directly in front of him.

"What-...er, who was that?" stammered Finn putting his sock and boot back on.

"That was him," replied the badger.

"Who's him?" asked Finn with a note of impatience at the suggestion that he should know who 'him' was.

"'Him that's been causing all the trouble I told you about yesterday, remember?"

Finn had absolutely no memory whatsoever of a conversation yesterday which included 'him'.

"Well I'll tell you again then, should I?" retorted the badger impatiently. "It started about a month ago. We noticed things were being moved like, not where they're supposed to be. Squirrels were getting wary and started complaining 'bout the same thing cos all their food stores for the winter were being spoilt. We had a meeting and in the end we decided to put out night watches in the areas where we knew it were happening. It were me that saw him first. He appeared in a flash he did, and started digging in the ground midway into the woods by the old oaks. I shouted to him I did. I shouted, 'Oi, what you looking for?' As soon as I shouted, he looked up and just vanished. Not a word or anything. Anyway, we noticed that holes were starting to appear all over the woods. They're taking stones of some sort away with them and we don't know how them people are getting here or where they're going. Oh and we know it's them cos we put two watches out one night at either end of the wood and both watches saw him- . . . or them."

"If he can vanish in a flash," said Finn, "how do you know it wasn't just him?"

Arnold scowled. "Now look here young whipper snapper, you're supposed to be helping us, not complicating things, alright?"

For a second time in two days it took a while for Finn to gather his senses. Arnold was now standing right in front of him on his hind legs with his paws on his hips. Any other time this sight might have appeared comical but at this particular moment it did not.

"I don't know what you want of me," said Finn looking down at his feet. "I've been coming to these woods all my life for as long as I can remember. I love it here and if I could help you I would."

Arnold surveyed Finn for another minute or so before he replied. "Look lad, we need you to come up here at night cos we reckon with our legs and your brains we can work this out together. We've been watching you grow up. Been following you round as you go through woods.

We know you love this place. That's why we want yer help."

Finn was no longer apprehensive of Arnold, whose voice had softened. He walked towards him. He noticed his fur was greying around his mouth, suggesting he was mature in years but his eyes were jet black and his stare was fixed on Finn.

"Why at night time?" asked Finn. "It must be mid morning by now and we saw the man!"

"They don't normally come out in daylight. Reckon that one had dropped whatever stuck in your foot and he had to get it back sharpish. Must have been important to him, so.... you'll help us then?"

Finn nodded.

At that moment there was a flurry of activity and animals emerged from every direction. The birds twittered ceaselessly, the squirrels ran back and forth along the branches and a small herd of deer scraped at the earth with their hooves.

"Now now then," came another familiar voice. Amelia was now standing by her husband's side. "Let him be now. We've got to make plans if we going to get this right."

The noise quietened down almost immediately and the animals stood still listening intently.

It was Finn who spoke first. "I'll come back tonight at midnight. Where should I meet you?" he asked, looking specifically at Arnold.

"'Here will do lad," and without another word, Arnold and Amelia turned and disappeared. The rest of the animals seemed to melt away into the undergrowth and Finn found himself entirely alone with not a single shred of evidence that the last half an hour had ever happened.

Chapter Three

The Travellers

After returning from the woods just before lunch, Finn took great care to avoid his mother as he washed the dried blood off his face. His nose had stopped bleeding but it was sore and his left eye was slightly swollen. He knew he couldn't hide his face away from her for too long and she would want to know what had happened. Although

Finn had no loyalty to Christian in any way, he felt it best to come up with an alternative tale, rather than his mother worrying that he was being bullied. Finn felt she had enough worries without him adding to them.

Later that afternoon Finn was in the garden sweeping up the first autumn leaves when a familiar noise caught his attention. He ran over to the garden wall which overlooked the main road through the village. The sound of pots and pans rattling, and the rhythmic clip clopping of hooves told Finn that the gypsies were coming to town. He felt a rush of excitement at the prospect of seeing Ryan, his gypsy friend again and the time they would spend playing in the woods together. Sure enough within a couple of minutes, a convoy of brightly painted caravans paraded past the cottage on their way to the field behind the village shop. The gypsies never stayed more than a couple of days and Finn thought this was probably due to the cold welcome from the other villagers. Finn smiled and waved enthusiastically as each caravan passed the cottage, unlike the other villagers who pulled their curtains and shut their doors.

Finn remembered his very first visit to the gypsy camp a couple of years ago when his mother had finally trusted him to go out alone to play. He had crouched under the hedge lying on his tummy, straining to see through the leaves. He had not heard Ryan and some of the other gypsy children creep up behind him, which was unusual as Finn's hearing was as sharp as a fox. Finn had expected the worst and put his hands over his face, the way he did at school when he was surrounded by Christian and his friends. The boys did not strike Finn, but took him by the arm and led him into the camp. As they approached the camp, the music and chatter stopped and Finn had felt quite uncomfortable as dozens of eyes were upon him. Within seconds the music began to play and the atmosphere buzzed once more. After some initial introductions Finn was made most welcome and Ryan soon become a firm friend.

Finn finished the rest of his chores as quickly as he could, and after eating his tea in record time, he made his way over the field at the back of the cottage, along the path by the brook and over the style into the field where the camp was. The dozen or so caravans had been parked in a circle and the horses were now tethered at the other end of the field, grazing contently. In the middle of the circle a large fire was already crackling away, shooting yellow and orange sparks up into the sky. A couple of the other children recognised Finn and shouted his name, smiling at him. Finn smiled back and made his way over to the caravan that Ryan and his family stayed in. It was painted bright red with a silver roof and had white lace curtains at the window. A line of green shamrocks had been painted around the metal window frame.

Finn knocked gently on the door calling Ryan's name. The door burst open and Ryan stood there, a smile stretched from ear to ear, his dark brown curly hair sprouting in every direction. Ryan's ripped shirt nearly made Finn feel well dressed, but Ryan's lifestyle and quest for adventure meant that clothes didn't last long at all.

Finn was welcomed into the caravan and shown the same warm hospitality he'd come to expect. Hot soup, warm buttered bread rolls and chocolate cake was handed out and even though Finn had eaten his tea, he couldn't resist the delicious flavours offered to him. As dusk fell, Ryan and Finn settled themselves by the brook not far from the camp fire, lying on their backs and chewing grass. Although they hadn't seen each other for nearly a year, it was like they had never been apart; they felt totally comfortable in each other's company. The scattered stars twinkled above them. The moon was in the shape of an arc, a yellow shadow seemed to surround it. In the background the sound of pipes, flutes and drums could be heard as the gypsies danced around the fire, singing their songs into the night. Finn deliberated whether or not to tell Ryan about his meeting with Arnold and Amelia in the woods earlier that day, or about the little man who had shouted at him for standing on the crystal pin.

"What happened to your face?" asked Ryan eventually. "Is that idiot Christian still giving you a hard time?"

Finn grimaced and nodded his head. "I usually keep out of his way. But I couldn't this morning cos there were three of them and they had all me escape routes covered."

"Where were you heading like?" inquired Ryan.

"I was going to the woods, you know where the sycamores are? I just wanted to check something out."

"Oh ay what might that be?" asked Ryan sitting up.

Finn knew he would either have to lie, or trust Ryan with his secret. He decided to tell his friend the truth.

"Wow," replied Ryan, his mouth open and the piece of grass dropped to the floor. "That's amazing. Do you think I could see them men and hear what the badgers are saying?"

"Not sure," replied Finn shrugging his shoulders. "But I'm meeting the badgers tonight at midnight to see if we can catch the little man and find out what's going on. Want to come?"

"Sure thing," said Ryan his voice full of excitement. "I'll wait for you by the wall at the back of your house," he shouted over his shoulder as he ran back towards the caravans.

Chapter Four

Night Watch

Later that night Finn lay quietly in his bed listening

for the 11:30 chime of the hall clock. It had not been easy

staying awake and he was sure he had dozed off a couple

of times. At last he heard the chime he had been waiting

for and crept out of bed. He was already fully clothed to

save time and to avoid making any unnecessary noise that

might wake his mother, who usually was tucked into her

own bed by 10pm. Finn had decided to exit the house through his bedroom window, out into the back garden and over the small stone wall which encircled the house. The garden was mostly laid to grass and Finn knew how to navigate across it quickly and avoid any obstacles. Ryan was already there, sitting on the wall waiting.

Once Finn had jumped the wall and the two boys had set off in the direction of the woods, Finn suddenly realised, that unlike the badgers, he did not have night vision and finding his way to the Old Sycamores in the pitch black was probably impossible. Fortunately for him, Arnold had also realised this and was waiting for him at the edge of the wood. Finn's expression was enough to tell Arnold he had done the right thing. Arnold carefully surveyed Ryan and then looked at Finn.

"It's OK," encouraged Finn, "This is Ryan. He's a good friend. We can trust him."

Ryan nodded his head at the badger as if trying to give more weight to Finn's statement. Arnold didn't reply, much to the disappointment of both the boys and took the lead into the woods. They walked in silence, Arnold on all fours and completely alert to every unfamiliar noise. The twigs snapped under their feet, and apart from a pale light from the moon, it was virtually impossible to see where they were going. The boys soon learned to follow directly behind Arnold to avoid bumping into trees and falling over broken branches or raised tree roots.

After about ten minutes they reached the ridge where Finn had been standing earlier that day. Amelia was already waiting for them and beckoned them both over to her hiding place behind a thick thorn bush. Finn quickly introduced Ryan to Amelia.

She smiled at the newcomer. "Hello Ryan, I've met some of your relatives in the past, here in these woods and I remember they treated me with kindness."

Ryan's face beamed and he nodded to Finn to signify he had heard every word. Arnold, Ryan and Finn sat down and watched for any movement around the trees. The squirrels and other inhabitants had all been told not to venture near tonight to avoid any false alarms. They sat in the dark in silence. The only sound was the water in the brook gurgling as it made its way over rocks and stones to the river and, finally, into the North Sea. Finn had spent many a pleasant afternoon in the spring sunshine fishing in this brook. As the time passed, Finn started to feel cold and wished he'd put an extra jersey on. He felt his head starting to fall forwards and the next thing he knew Amelia was gently shaking him awake.

"Listen dear, you two may as well go back home. He's not going to show up now and if he does, well we'll have missed him. We'll try again tomorrow."

Arnold escorted Finn and Ryan back to the edge of the wood, walking once again in complete silence until they stopped at the slope just before the road into the village.

"See you tomorrow, 'bout same time?"

"Yes I suppose so," replied Finn with a yawn.

"Definitely," said Ryan.

"Sorry you didn't see nothing," said Finn after Arnold had left them.

"Ah, it was brilliant," smiled Ryan, "And Jezus, I heard them badgers talk. What could be more exciting than that?"

Ryan and Finn parted company at the garden wall where they had met. Finn climbed back through his window and fell into bed without bothering to undress. He heard no more chimes from the clock and fell into a deep slumber.

Chapter Five

A Day in the Wood

Early the next morning, the church bells could be heard ringing from Meersbrook, the next village. Tyndale didn't have its own church so people had to walk the one and half miles if they wanted to attend the Sunday service. Finn and his mother had never attended the Sunday service, or any other service for that matter. Weddings, funerals and christenings all took place there, but Finn and his mother had not been included in the village activities since the death of his father.

Finn ambled down the lane feeling relaxed and looking forward to the day ahead. As he climbed the style he saw Ryan walking towards him, wearing the same cheeky, boyish grin he always wore.

"Ready to explore?" asked Finn, holding up his fishing rod.

"You betcha," laughed Ryan, holding up a small bag full of food in return.

The boys walked up the field, following the brook so as to avoid the main road and the villagers as they walked to church. Archie, Ryan's small black and white terrier, followed closely at their heels, sniffing at every tree. At the end of the field they crawled through a gap in a hawthorn hedge, climbed up a steep slope and found themselves at the edge of the west side of the wood, not far from the base of the mountain. They followed the path which meandered its way down to a rock plateau and finally to a flat grassy area by the brook. The sound of a waterfall cascading down the rock face could be heard not far away. The boys settled themselves down to fish. There were large white boulders at the water's edge which made excellent seats. Ryan cast his line into the water.

"Want to light a fire?" asked Ryan staring into the water, straining his eyes to see if there were any fish swimming about and seeing nothing but his own reflection. Finn nodded and started to collect dry twigs and leaves. He felt in his pocket and took out a small box of matches. He and Ryan had explored the woods on many occasions and he knew beforehand what he needed to bring with him.

Soon a small fire burned on the grass. Finn placed a circle of stones around the hot ashes to contain the fire from spreading any further. It wasn't long before both boys were hungry. Finn had brought cold bacon sandwiches and a lump of cheddar cheese. Ryan opened his bag and took out two home baked fruit scones, two apples and a bottle of ginger ale. Archie sat expectantly at Finn's side knowing that if any food was to come his way, it would come from him. After they had demolished every last morsel of food, they lay on their backs looking at the ever changing shapes of the clouds as they stretched their way across the sky. The sun found its way through gaps in the clouds and still gave some warmth despite autumn being well underway.

"What's it like?" asked Finn. "Being a traveller?"

"It's alright I suppose," replied Ryan. "I can't really say cos me family have always travelled, so I don't know any other way. Nor do me parents, cos they've always been travellers too. It's in the blood I guess. Sometimes I think I'd like to stay in a place a bit longer, maybe go to school for a while. But that's not our way. If we stay in a place too long, the local council come knocking, wanting to put us on official sites and saying us kids should go to school. That's not what me mam and dad want, so we just keep going."

"Do you do any school work?"

"You mean can I read and write?" laughed Ryan. "Of course I can. Me mam sees to that. We got books and stuff you know. I can do me sums too. Maybe not as good as you, but I know enough to get me by."

A large black cloud hid the sun and the boys decided to move on. They cleared up the rubbish and burnt it on the fire before carefully stamping out the flames with their feet. They headed up the rocky ridge in front of them, keeping to the path by the side of the waterfall and towards the base of the mountain. Here the narrow pathway, now lined with tall ferns, swung westward once again towards the setting sun. The boys hadn't been this way before and were keen to see where the path would lead them. A cool east wind had started to blow and Finn buttoned up his jacket. They followed the path until it split into a fork. They deliberated for a moment before taking the right hand path between two crevices. The opening was tight and they had to squeeze in sideward. Just on the other side of the crevice was the mouth of a cave. Finn took out the matches and lit one. The cave was dark and the light from the match sent shadows ricocheting from wall to wall. As their eyes scanned their surroundings, they knew they weren't the first visitors to this cave. Black ashes from a fire lay in a small pile. A broken fishing rod lay discarded next to a pair of worn-looking, black leather boots.

The boys looked at one another understanding each other's thoughts. Not only had somebody visited here, they had lived here for a while. Ryan walked over to the fire and picked up one of the stones. He etched his name into the rock wall along with the date of his birthday. He turned and smiled at Finn who picked up his own stone and did the same.

"See these," said Ryan pointing to the freshly made marks in the stone, "reckon they'll be here forever. Betcha!"

Outside, a storm was brewing. The wind was now whipping around the mouth of the cave and large raindrops pattered furiously onto the rocks outside. Finn put his head out and looked up at the dark sky.

"Shouldn't last long," he said. "I think we should stay in here until it's passed."

Ryan nodded his head in agreement and sat down on one of the larger rocks by the burnt out fire, listening to the rain falling steadily outside. Finn picked up the old boots, looking for any clues as to their owner.

"Know when you're coming back to Tyndale?" he asked without looking at Ryan.

"I don't know. Me dad never says nowt 'bout where we're going. It might be in a couple of months or it might be next year. We don't like coming here that often cos of the other villagers."

Finn nodded his head in an understanding way. "Just imagine how I feel," he thought out loud.

Ryan didn't say anything and continued to make shapes in the gravel with a stick.

"You know Tyndale aint the worst place we've been to," said Ryan eventually breaking the silence. "We've had worse than dirty looks and snide remarks."

Finn looked over at Ryan giving him his full attention.

"We went to this one place, can't remember the name, but it were up north not far from the borders. They hated us there. Me mam wouldn't let me go out of the camp that night for fear of them lynching me."

"What happened," asked Finn intrigued but suddenly realising that human intolerance existed beyond the borders of Tyndale.

"They shouted at us as we took tack off the horses. Told us to get lost and never come back. We thought that were it, but when we got up next morning, two of the dogs were lying dead, still tied up."

"What had they done to them?" asked Finn, now beginning to visualise a horrible scene in his head.

"Poisoned – rat poison. We left as soon as it were light and never went back."

"Guess the villagers won that one then, didn't they?" said Finn, suddenly feeling sorry for Ryan and his fellow travellers. He hoped that the villagers in Tyndale would never stoop to behaving so badly.

"It's not always like that," said Ryan noticing the sadness on Finn's face. "Some places are great, where we get a good welcome and we know they'll be glad to see us."

Finn nodded his head and smiled in appreciation at Ryan's attempt to make him feel better.

When the storm had passed and the sky cleared, the boys retraced their steps back through the wood until they eventually reached the hawthorn hedge near the bridge at the entrance to the village. Just before they went their separate ways, Ryan paused, fumbling in his pocket.

"I wanted to give you this." He held out his hand and dropped something cold and hard into Finn's palm. "It's for good luck and means the angels will be watching over you."

Finn had read about angels in the bible, but he had never heard anybody talk about them before and the mere mention of them stirred his imagination. He looked down and admired the small brass shamrock in his hand

"I've nothing to give you," said Finn, still staring into his palm.

"I didn't give it you for somet back," laughed Ryan turning to go.

"Wait," shouted Finn. He walked over to a holly bush abundant with red berries. On the top of the bush sat a single white feather swaying precariously in the wind. He walked over to Ryan and held out his hand. "I know it's not much – but maybe you could keep it?"

Ryan took the feather and smiled. "Wow, me mam says these mean there are big changes coming, for the one who finds it. That means you Finn, but I'll keep it for you just the same."

Feeling much better, Finn waved to Ryan and made his way back home.

Chapter Six

In the Thicket of Things

Two more nights of sneaking out and sitting at various points around the woods followed. There were no sightings of the mysterious man looking for pebbles. Finn was getting extremely tired and had been scolded at school for daydreaming and falling asleep during a reading lesson. He knew that if he carried on like this, his school teachers were sure to inform his mother that he wasn't getting enough sleep, and she would start asking him questions. Finn had always enjoyed more freedom than most of the other children in the village to wander freely through the woods and the fields. He didn't want to do anything that might result in that freedom being curtailed, especially while the gypsies were still around. It was alright for Ryan, thought Finn, who had joined in on the night watches. He never had to worry about wearing school uniform or going to school, ever. He briefly tried to imagine what it must be like to live the way Ryan and his family did. The thought definitely appealed to him but he knew that his mother would not even consider moving into the next village a few miles away, let alone travelling constantly from town to town.

Finn was also taking care to avoid Christian and his cronies. Finn's black eye after the fist fight had caused the other children to whisper under their breath as they walked past him in the school yard. Christian had smiled at his handiwork, his friends quietly encouraging him to carry out a repeat performance. Fortunately for Finn, the arrival of a new toy called, a pogo stick, took Christian's attention away from punching Finn for a second time. The children queued up impatiently, pushing and shoving themselves forwards to try and get a go of the new device before the school bell rang, indicating that lessons were about to start again.

After the third night watch there was still no sight of the little man and the boys were escorted back to the edge of the woods. Ryan and Arnold had got over the initial awkwardness between them and now chatted quite happily, Ryan telling Arnold about the badgers he had seen in other parts of the country. A few metres from the edge of the wood Arnold stopped suddenly and stood up on his hind legs. A commotion could be heard coming from the direction of the gypsy camp. The two boys ran as fast as their legs would carry them towards the field. To Finn's horror, some of the villagers had surrounded the camp and were throwing stones at the horses. They shouted names and waved their fire torches in the air, slowly moving forwards towards the camp. The gypsies were out of their caravans armed with sticks in an attempt to ward off the villagers. The horses neighed furiously, rearing up into the air trying to break free from the mayhem. Albert Shuttleswaite was nowhere to be seen and Finn knew he would stay well clear of any trouble like this.

Finn watched the commotion and wondered what he could do. He wasn't the most popular boy in the village so anything he might say to try and bring peace would probably have an adverse effect. Ryan grabbed Finn's arm and pulled him out of view. The boys crouched low in a ditch and waited. After a while the noise started to quieten down. Footsteps and muffled voices could be heard passing them by as the villagers returned to their cottages, some cursing and swearing about the trouble the gypsies had brought to the village. It occurred to Finn that the only people, who weren't causing trouble, were the gypsies themselves.

Ryan turned to face Finn. "Look Finn, I'm going have to get going. Mam will be right worried 'bout me now and I'll have to tell her I've been out with you. She won't be best pleased 'bout me sneaking out, but don't worry it'll be me that'll get the hiding – not you!"

He smiled, patted Finn on the shoulder and sprinted out of the ditch back towards the red and silver van.

Finn walked home and jumped the wall into the darkness of the garden. He climbed through the window and fell onto the bed. The springs creaked as he landed on the mattress. As soon as his head hit the pillow, the bedroom light came on. His mother was stood in the doorway, her pink flannelette dressing gown zipped up to her neck.

"Where've you been?" she demanded, her arms firmly folded.

Finn had to think quickly as he wasn't sure if his mother knew how long he had actually been out.

"I heard noises outside, people shouting, and I knew there was going be trouble, so I got up and followed everyone up the road." He stared at his mother. She made no attempt to reply so Finn spoke again. "Look," he explained, "I was worried 'bout Ryan. I'm sorry, I know I should've asked you first."

His mother looked slightly more appeased at his explanation. Her body seem to relax and she unfolded her arms. "Is he OK, Ryan?"

"I think so. Some folk threw stones, others made a noise but they've all gone home now. I'll speak to Ryan in the morning."

"Ay, and I'll speak to you in the morning," she said before closing the door and going back to bed.

The next morning Finn was up early, despite getting only a few hours sleep. He wanted to visit Ryan before his mother got out of bed, just on the off chance she would keep him indoors. This had only ever happened to Finn once that he could remember and it was a result of him forgetting to shut the chicken hut door before he went to bed. Not one single chicken was alive the next day, their carcasses strewn around the coop. That oversight had deprived them of eggs and fresh meat for the next month or so.

Finn opened the chicken hut door as he did every morning, and made his way up to the camp to see how much damage had been done. When he reached the field it was empty. Not one single caravan. The only sign that there had been anyone in the field at all, was some flattened grass and several black rocks still lying on the ground. Finn felt a strange feeling in the pit of his stomach. Why hadn't Ryan come to say goodbye? Finn knew the answer to his own question, and understood that the gypsies had probably left before dawn to avoid any more trouble, and Ryan wouldn't have had the chance to visit Finn. He walked back to the cottage, anger simmering away inside of him. He was more determined than ever to leave this village as soon as he was old enough to, and take his mother with him.

The villagers congratulated themselves at the disappearance of the gypsies and village life quickly got back to normal.

Finn tried to talk to his mother about what had happened but she had just waved her hand in the air and said, "Finn, you know what the folks are like round here. There's nothing we can do 'bout it. You just keep your head down and stay out of trouble will you? Don't want that lot knocking on my door."

She then scolded him for leaving the house in the middle of the night but that had been the end of the matter, much to Finn's relief.

Finn tried to keep his mind off what had happened by focusing on helping the badgers. In order to ensure his mother didn't notice he was missing, he put pillows and rolled up clothes under the blankets in case she popped her head around the door. It was on the sixth night of duty with the badgers that any real breakthrough came. After about an hour sitting under the wooden bridge between Badgers Hollow and Bramble Way, a strange scuffling noise could be heard. This was followed by a splash and string of curses. Finn drew his breath in anticipation and watched the branches of a holly bush being shoved to one side. He recognised the little man as he appeared out from the bush nursing newly acquired scratches. In his hand he held a small trowel that shone in the moonlight. Unaware of his audience he started to scrape away the earth from the bottom of a tree. He muttered to himself, stopping occasionally to scratch his head. After about five minutes, the digging stopped and the man took a white pebble out of the earth, grasped it tightly in his hand and held it up to the moon. He chanted the same indecipherable word three times and then put the pebble in his pocket. It was at this moment Finn decided to make the first move.

"Excuse me sir," he said quietly and in the most unassuming way he could. "Please could you tell us- er me, what you're looking for?"

The man jumped backwards in surprise and turned to face Finn. He looked him up and down wearing the same scowl he had worn on their first meeting.

"What may I ask, are you doing out of bed?"

Finn had not expected to be reprimanded by this strange little man for being out of bed.

"I came to see you sir," replied Finn. "I met you the other day and I-"

"And you what?" came the sharp reply.

"Well I wanted to ask you some questions about what that thing was that stuck in my foot and what you wanted it for."

"Very inquisitive boy aren't you?" said the man still staring at Finn. "If you must know, I am working. This is my job," and he continued to dig.

"Collecting pebbles is a job?"

"Yes! And a very important job at that."

The man stopped digging, stood up and stared at Finn.

"Where're you taking them?"

"To the mountain over there," replied the little man as he pointed northwest towards the mountain Finn had always known as Mount Shallien.

Finn opened his mouth to speak again but the man spoke before he could.

"No, that's enough questions for one night. Off you go to bed."

"But I-"

"You heard me, off to bed."

The man vanished on the spot leaving Finn's mouth open in mid-sentence.

"Well that went well, didn't it?" Arnold's voice cut through the darkness.

"Well I think it did," said Amelia. "At least we know now where they're taking the pebbles."

It was agreed that there would be no more sightings that night and that everyone should go home, it was now nearly dawn. Arnold escorted Finn to the edge of the wood. After waving goodbye, Finn slid down the grass track towards the road, a noise behind him quickly made him turn. He listened and heard the noise again. Curious, he retraced his steps back to the trees. The birds were just starting to welcome the new day with their dawn chorus. Finn stood and listened. The leaves rustled in the branches. Suddenly, Christian came flying out of a tree and landed on top of Finn, squashing him face down into the ground.

"Where've you 'been?" hissed Christian down Finn's ear. "I've been following you these past couple of nights. What you up to Tink?"

Finn struggled to get free but to no avail as Christian was almost twice his size.

"If you let go of me, I'll tell you," lied Finn, as he had no intention of telling Christian anything.

"Bloody right you will." replied Christian now yanking a handful of hair out of Finn's head.

The next few moments happened quickly. Finn felt the weight being lifted off him and heard a deep growling voice shouting, "Be off with you. Yer young scaly wag."

Christian took one look at the tramp, screamed and ran down the grass track, down the road towards the village, not daring to look behind him. Finn lifted his head, and there in front of him stood Old Tom.

"'An' you," carried on Tom, as he took Finn's collar and yanked him up, "can come with me."

Chapter Seven

Old Tom

Finn found himself being dragged firmly along by Old Tom's side, back into the woods. After a couple of minutes of weaving in and out of the trees, they stood before the wooden shack that Tom lived in. Tom shoved Finn roughly through the door before shutting it behind him.

"You know you're going to have to be a damn sight more discreet boy if you think you're going to get away with this!"

Finn stood still, looking up at the brown, weather beaten face peering down at him. He could taste blood in his mouth and he knew his lip was cut.

"Get away with what exactly?" replied Finn trying not to sound unnerved.

Tom turned and removed the dark brown, wide rimmed leather hat off his head, unveiling a head of scruffy black hair, the black being scattered with grey. He unbuttoned his coat and started to empty the pockets. Finn watched as he took out string, a small hammer, a hunting knife, some matches – it was endless and he wondered how on earth all the objects which now covered the table, ever fitted into two overcoat pockets.

"I think you and me ought to get a few things straight." said Tom filling a kettle with water from a jug and placing it on a hook over the fire. He motioned to Finn to sit on a wooden bench near the flames and away from the chill of the dawn air. He poured the hot water into two cups and handed one to Finn. Finn looked at the dark brown liquid before lifting the cup to his lips.

"Go on yer dafty – it won't kill you!" laughed Tom whose mood seemed to have lifted substantially after having a hot drink inside of him. Finn tasted the liquid. It was bitter and his taste buds recoiled, causing him to screw up his nose.

"Just coffee with some whiskey," laughed Tom at the expression on Finn's face. "Now, like I said, I think you and me ought to have a chat."

Finn opened his mouth to speak but Tom lifted his hand in such a way that Finn's mouth closed again.

"I've been living in these woods for some years now, and I've seen just 'bout everything there is to see, including you. I know you visit here regular, I know yer favourite place to sit and," he paused, "I know yer friends with that old badger and his wife."

Finn sat silently watching Tom. His face was covered with hair. His eye brows were almost as bushy as his beard. As he stared, Finn noticed Tom's eyes. They were the bluest eyes he had ever seen and Finn felt like he was looking into the doorway of a deep tunnel.

After a few moments Tom started to speak again.

"You aint like most of the boys round here. You're different. If you weren't, you wouldn't be able to hear what them badgers were saying or see them little men from the mountain. Most humans can't do those things, so don't go fretting that idiot Christian is going blow the whistle, cos he aint. He didn't see or hear nothing."

"He said he'd been following me," said Finn.

"Nah, he aint been following you. He aint brave enough to wander round woods at night. My guess is that he thought he would come early this morning to do some investigating for himself.... Don't think he'll be back in a hurry though." smiled Tom. "Anyhow, you've still got to be careful that you don't attract too much attention. Otherwise, they'll be folk traipsing all over these woods and neither of us wants that. Do we?"

"Ryan could hear the badgers too," whispered Finn.

"Ay, he's a different kettle of fish an' all that one. He's been brought up that way, to respect nature and the like."

"What 'bout you?" asked Finn now starting to feel a bit braver. "Guess you can hear them too!"

Tom looked down at his coffee, his hands encircling the cup. Eventually he looked up at Finn. "Yeah," he replied, "I can hear them."

Finn attempted to drink more of the coffee before it went cold. He looked around the shack and was surprised how homely Tom had managed to make it look. Animal skins hung on the walls and two lay on the floor as rugs.

74

On one wall there was a small shelf full of books, some of which Finn recognised, like the book about woodland trees and the sinking of the Titanic, and some he'd never heard of. The fire was crackling in the hearth and in the corner of the room was a wooden bed with one pillow and a couple of blankets.

"It's not much," said Tom watching Finn survey his surroundings, "But its home to me."

It was at this point that Finn decided that there was absolutely no point in hiding the truth from Tom and told him the story from the beginning.

"You know it's an honour, to be trusted by the animals in that way." said Tom.

Finn shrugged his shoulders. He certainly didn't feel honoured at this moment in time. He still had a black eye, a cut lip and his ribs hurt from being crushed by Christian.

"So, what you going to do?" asked Tom. "Keep helping them?"

"I can't stop now," replied Finn. "I've come this far and I want to know what's going on as much as the badgers do."

Tom smiled at Finn and the boy suddenly felt peaceful and at ease in this man's company. Finn didn't know much about Tom or his past. He had only heard the tales of the mad man in the woods who chased little children. It had never put Finn off visiting the woods and he realised that Tom had probably kept himself away from Finn as much as he could over the years so as not to frighten him. It also occurred to Finn that some of the older villagers knew more about Tom and how he had been unfairly treated by the mine, than they were willing to let on. Maybe, he thought, they were worried they'd end up in the same situation – homeless and unemployed – if they spoke out in his defence.

"Did you see what happened to the gypsies?" asked Finn.

"Yeah, I saw alright. Bloody imbeciles some of the folk who live here. Can't stand the thought of anyone being different. That's why you and me aint liked either. You know that don't you?"

Finn nodded his head. Yes he knew that. He had always known that but as Finn had been born in the village, it was all they could do to scorn him and ignore the antics of Christian and his pals. Finn knew his life in Tyndale would never be easy, not unless something changed; something that would sweep away the small mindedness that seemed to engulf the village and everyone in it.

"Tell you what," said Tom breaking into Finn's thoughts. "It gets pretty lonely in these woods, even with that badger and his misses gabbling on. Promise me you'll visit and keep me up to date with what's going on. And, if that Christian gives you any more bother, just mention I might be giving him a visit one of these dark nights! His pa holds no threat to me anymore."

Finn nodded his head and stood up to leave. Tom didn't move and Finn took this as a sign that the conversation was over, and it was definitely time to go. He buttoned his jacket as far as it would go and set out into the early morning sunshine back towards the village, his bedroom and warm, comfortable bed.

Chapter Eight

Images of the Past

It wasn't long before the weather changed. The watery autumn sun took its leave and was replaced by howling gales and torrential rain. Finn gazed out of the kitchen window. He knew any explorations around the woods would be impossible today. A fire burned in the cooking range and the room felt warm and cosy. His mother was in the kitchen baking bread. She looked over at Finn.

"You know today would be a good day to start clearing out that shed," she said kneading the dough with her fists. "I've asked you dozens of times now."

At the bottom of the garden there was an old rickety shed with a corrugated iron roof. Finn's mother had asked Finn on several occasions to clean it out and take out anything that they might be able to sell. Most of the items in there belonged to his father who had been a practical man and enjoyed making things. Finn still had the wooden trike that his father had made for him for his third birthday. Although he'd grown out of it some years ago, he just couldn't throw it away. Finn sighed and decided he couldn't put it off any longer. He grabbed his coat, pulled it over his head and battled his way down the garden path against the weather.

Inside, the shed smelt damp and musty. The walls were lined with shelves which were covered with tools and other rusty objects, most of which Finn didn't recognise or know the names of. He lit the small oil lamp and looked around. In one corner of the shed stood a pile of wooden boxes. He took a screwdriver off the shelf and prised the lid off the top box. The box fell to the ground and the contents fell out onto the stone floor. Finn picked up a heavy, dark coloured overcoat, work trousers and boots. He recognised them as mining gear and knew they must be the clothes his father had gone to work in. He pulled out two shirts and a waist coat and put them to one side. He took down the next box and once again prised open the lid. More clothes filled the box. He took out each item, inspecting it in the dim light. His mother had put all his father's belongings in here after his death. Underneath the clothes Finn could see paper and envelopes.

He opened a large brown envelope. It was covered in stains and ripped at the edges. Inside were his father's school reports from Tyndale Village School. It was the same school Finn went to. His father had been born in Tyndale. Finn's grandfather had also worked down the mine and it was expected that Finn's father would do the same as was village tradition. Finn read the reports. He smiled at the comments which described his father as being capable but absent minded about his school work. He took out a small handmade wooden box. Inside were black and white photographs. There was a picture of his father in school shorts and a woollen jacket, his school bag slung over his shoulder. His hair was as unruly as Finn's and his knees were grazed. Finn didn't know much about his father or his grandparents, and his mother conveniently changed the subject if Finn ever tried to talk about them.

Finn's mother had been born in Meersbrook and met his father at a dance in the village hall. People never travelled far from home and most of the villagers in the surrounding areas were related to someone in some way. She had moved into Tyndale leaving her elderly parents behind. Finn couldn't remember any of his grandparents. His grandfather on his mother's side of the family had died when he was a baby, and his grandmother died shortly afterwards. He remembered his mother saying it was because of a broken heart.

Finn had been named after his father's grandfather, Finbar O'Connor, who had left Ireland during the potato famine and travelled to London, before finally settling in Tyndale. Finn knew there were photographs somewhere of his parents' marriage with both sets of grandparents on them. When asked, his mother had shaken her head, saying she couldn't remember where they were and Finn had never broached the subject again.

Finn continued to empty the envelope. He took out another photograph. It was of his father at about the age of eight with another boy in his early teens. Finn did not recognise the boy, and had never seen any photos of him before. Both boys were smiling and the elder one had his arm around his father's shoulders. He put the photo in his trouser pocket determined at some point in the near future to ask his mother more questions.

At the bottom of the box was a sketch pad. On the front page was a sketch of a badger. A word had been scribbled underneath the drawing, which Finn couldn't make out. The badger was stood on his hind legs looking directly in front of him. It reminded Finn of Arnold when he stood that way. He flicked over the pages and the pad was full of sketches, not only of badgers, but of places in the woods that Finn recognised.

It wasn't long before Finn heard his mother shouting him in for tea. He tidied away his father's belongings and headed towards the house. They sat at the table eating in silence, Finn fingering the photograph in his pocket. He looked at his mother ready to bring up the question of what he'd found in the box. His mother looked tired and snapped her replies when he asked her mundane questions about her day. He decided to leave any questions about his father for a later date.

By late afternoon the sky had cleared and Finn took the opportunity to escape from the house. He took his usual route into the woods and knocked on the badger's door. Amelia smiled and beckoned him to crawl down the passageway into the small living room. Arnold was sat in an armchair in front of the fire.

"Well, this is an unexpected visit," he said turning to face Finn.

"I wanted to ask you something," said Finn, pulling the sketches of the badgers he had found in the box, out of his jacket pocket. "Did you know my pa?" he said, handing one of the hand drawn sketches to Arnold.

Arnold looked at the sketch. "Nay, lad, I've never met yer pa. But that's my grandfather in this picture here. His name were Albert."

Finn's sat back and stared at Arnold, waiting for more information. Amelia sat quietly at the table also looking at Arnold, waiting for him to speak.

"Yer pa were just like you," said Arnold fidgeting on his chair. "He used to wander round these woods just like you do now. He could hear us animals and became a good friend to me granddad. That's why I weren't surprised when you fell through door that day. And I knew you'd be able to hear me. Come to think of it, I did wonder why you were so shocked. Thought you'd know 'bout family gift... Anyway, once your pa got a bit older like, he stopped visiting the woods and started working down that mine. He seemed to forget everything he'd ever seen or learnt in the woods. My grandpa never saw him again."

Finn did not speak so Arnold continued.

"You're a chip off the old block you are, although.....
me and Amelia like, well we were hoping that you wouldn't
forget 'bout us as quick as yer pa forgot 'bout his friends."

Finn reached into his pocket again and took out the
photograph. He gave it to Arnold.

"Do you know who this is, with my pa?"

"Has yer ma never told you owt like?" said Arnold,
looking at the photograph and shaking his head. "Guess
she don't want to open old wounds now, and it has been a
long time since it happened."

"Since what happened?" retorted Finn, now
concerned that secrets had been kept from him.

"Look lad, this aint my place and I won't say no
more. Seems there were a lot of history in that box you
opened... There is someone who can tell you 'bout yer pa
much better than I ever could."

"Who?" asked Finn. "Do they still live here, in
Tyndale?"

"You already know the answer to both those questions lad."

Sensing that Arnold had no intention of discussing the matter further, Finn grabbed his coat and walked home, his mind entwined with thoughts about what mysteries he had yet to discover about his family, and why his mother was so reluctant to speak about it.

Chapter Nine

A Knock on the Window

Throughout these events Finn found it more difficult than usual to concentrate at school. It had not gone unnoticed and his teacher Mrs. Kirkwood had asked Finn on several occasions if he was feeling unwell. He knew he must hide his tiredness - which was now mingled with excitement after his brief conversation with the little man - if his secret was to remain one. He also felt a relief from being able to tell Tom what was going on and felt he had an ally, not only against Christian, who was now going to great lengths to avoid Finn, but with the whole night watch saga in the woods.

Ever since his conversation with Arnold, Finn had stared at some of the villagers and then checked the photograph still in his trouser pocket. He wondered more and more who the person was, and if he was still alive. Perhaps he would be able to give him the answers about his father's past that had so far eluded him. Finn hadn't seen anyone who looked remotely like the boy in the picture, although, he knew that the boy would be a grown man by now and it would be difficult to recognise him.

Finn also thought about the mountain where the pebbles were being taken. Mount Shallien was also known locally as 'Fairy Mountain' and had been for generations. It had an unusual amount of rose quartz crystal embedded in the rock, and in the evenings as the sun set in the western sky, the top of the mountain shimmered with a pinkish glow, which mixed with the deep reds from the setting sun. Tales were told of the healing properties in the natural spring waters that ran freely down the sides of the mountain.

His mind was suddenly jolted back into the classroom by Mrs Kirkwood wrapping his knuckles with her ruler and giving him a half an hour detention after school for daydreaming.

Two nights after the meeting with the little man, Finn asked Arnold for a night off. He was feeling exhausted and knew that a good night's sleep was necessary if he was to avoid any more trouble at school or at home. Arnold had agreed after some pressure from Amelia and organised another watch to cover Finn's absence. Finn excused himself to his very surprised mother who could not ever remember Finn asking to go to bed at nine o'clock. He collapsed into his bed and fell into a deep restful sleep.

He was awakened by a tapping noise. He lay still, not sure whether he had heard the noise at all. There it was again, a tapping noise on his window. Finn sat up and pulled back the curtain. Outside his window were four men who looked very similar to the little man he had met in the woods. Like him, they were dressed in tunics of gold and green, belted round the middle.

Quietly he opened the window.

"Good evening, young sir," said the one at the front. "We've come to answer your questions, so you'd better put your coat on, as it's quite chilly out here."

Excited, and getting quite used to strange and unexpected occurrences, Finn quickly put on his coat and climbed out of the bedroom window.

"Where are you taking me and how did you know where I lived?"

"It was decided by one of the elders that your curiosity and determination over the last week deserved some answers," replied the same man.

"Over the last week? How do you know what I've been doing over the last week?"

The man smiled. "You do not always have to see in order to know. My name is Geroma and I am pleased to make your acquaintance. Please follow us."

Finn duly obeyed and followed the four men as they moved off in the direction of the mountain. Each man carried a small lantern which glowed enough to cast light on the path in front of them. Finn noticed that the flame was not yellow but silver and did not flicker at all. So many questions were popping into his head, but the men were not speaking and he decided that any questions would have to wait. His stomach growled with a combination of hunger and excitement. He could hear his heart thumping in his rib cage. He looked around as he walked through the woods to see if he could spot Arnold or Amelia, or Tom, but

all was quiet and no one and nothing stirred that night.

Chapter Ten

Mount Shallien

The party walked through the woods until they reached the base of the mountain. In front of them was a very large stone. Geroma, the leader of the group, stepped forward and placed the palm of his left hand over a triangular mark on the stone. A rumbling noise could be heard from inside the wall and then the stone seemed to dissolve in front of Finn's eyes. He followed them into a well-lit chamber, and behind them the stone materialised once again to form an impenetrable barrier between them and the outside world.

The chamber felt warm, and on the walls were several lanterns all glowing with the same silver light. Finn was ushered to the front of the group where another man appeared in front of him.

"Welcome, Finn. We are honoured to have you here as our visitor. It has been many moons since we have had human visitors inside this mountain. My name is Karibar and I am going to be your guide this evening."

Karibar walked down a narrow corridor and beckoned Finn to follow him. "I know you have many questions Finn. I can hear them in your head. I will talk to you as we walk and hopefully most of them will be answered."

Finn was becoming aware that these men had the ability to read his thoughts and made a mental note to try and be careful to concentrate only on finding out what he wanted to know.

After a few minutes Karibar spoke again. "You are inside Mount Shallien. This is a very sacred place. I and the others you have met are part of an ancient race. We have lived here since the beginning of the mountain's existence. We do not grow physically older. There is no time in this mountain as such. Although we are aware of your seasons and years passing outside, they do not penetrate these walls or affect our outward appearance. This mountain is a doorway to other realms of existence."

Karibar smiled and Finn knew immediately he had heard the question that he wanted to ask.

"No Finn, we do not class ourselves as aliens. We like to think of ourselves as interplanetary beings, and we are the custodians of this doorway."

They walked on and entered another chamber which was similar to the last only warmer still.

"We are going further into the mountain's core as this is where the main activity of our work is carried out. It will get warmer as we get nearer to the volcanic fires, which burn in the heart of the mountain. Without these volcanoes the planet would have ceased to exist further than what you call the Ice Age."

Finn was led over to a wooden platform which descended unaided down a narrow tunnel and stopped at another chamber deeper within the mountain. The silver lanterns were everywhere and lit up the scene all around. Each chamber they visited was full of the little men scurrying about fulfilling their duties. At no time did Finn feel frightened or worried as he was transported from one part of the mountain to another. Once the platform had stopped, Karibar stepped out into the chamber and led Finn by the hand. Finn was immediately aware of sound.

There was singing and instruments playing the most divine music he had ever heard. As the music filled his head, he felt a tingling sensation in the whole of his body, as if every atom of his being was vibrating in harmony with the sound. It filled the deep silence, and as Finn looked up, a rainbow of colour stretched out above him. He thought of the Northern Lights he had read about in geography lessons and wondered if they looked like this. He knew that some time in the future he would have to travel to the north to see these magnificent lights for himself.

Finn was just about to ask Karibar if he was one of the elders who had been spoken of by Geroma, when Karibar spoke again.

"No Finn, I am not one of the elders. They oversee our work here, and there are only five of them. You will meet them in due course."

Finn looked around the chamber and opened his mouth to speak but no words came. The wall opposite was filled with hundreds of lines of crystal pins. Finn recognised the pins as being the same as the one he had stepped on earlier that week. Inside the pins a diamond-filled liquid bubbled away. Supporting the structure of pins were rows of white pebbles, each one giving off a silver shadow in the semi-darkness.

"This is called the energiser." Karibar spoke softly at Finn's side. "It is a support system for this planet you humans refer to as Earth. Earth is also known by the name of Gaia by interplanetary beings, and, by some human beings who have a deeper understanding of the universe. Regrettably, there are also humans who do not share this understanding, and believe that this planet belongs to them to do with as they deem appropriate. This is not so.

"Gaia does not belong to mankind. She is an individual consciousness or entity within the solar system. She works in harmony with her brothers and sisters in the night sky to maintain the fine balance necessary to allow all life forms to continue to exist. Each planet and star in every solar system work together in full knowledge of each other's existence and importance.

"Gaia has suffered terribly at the hands of her human inhabitants. Over time, wars, pollution and the continued destruction of forests and other natural resources, have resulted in imbalances that have needed to be attended to. Sometimes Gaia takes her own action and by the very force of her nature causes what humans see as catastrophic natural disasters. But we see them as a new beginning. And, as we all originate from the same energy source and we are all connected; we are all affected in some way.

"We, as custodians also have our role to play in ensuring the survival of Gaia. The energiser creates a force field using natural minerals and liquids to replenish the planet's energy stores during periods of weakness. This enables the planet to heal herself. It is our job to keep the energiser working at all times and at full capacity. The white pebbles we collect are made from a unique crystal compound. They lose their power every eon or so, and have to be replaced. As a rule, we are invisible to the human eye and our presence is only perceived by the animals that live in the woods. You have proved yourself to be an exception, hence the elders' decision to invite you into the mountain."

Finn stood and stared at the energiser and no words or thoughts came to him. He did, however, sense that the words he had just been told made complete sense.

After a brief moment of silence, Karibar nodded and continued to answer the question that had popped inside Finn's head.

"No, this is not the only energiser on the planet. Another energiser lies in the depths of the mountains in the south of New Zealand. The land is similar to here and able to provide a plentiful store of natural resources. There, members of the same race as us work as tirelessly as we

do. Come Finn, it is now time for you to meet the elders."

Chapter Eleven

The Elders

Finn was led out of the chamber and onto the platform again. The platform moved first downwards and then horizontally further into the mountain. The temperature was getting warmer, and it was Karibar who spoke first.

"The elders are very sensitive and require a constant temperature. It is only in the centre of the mountain that this can be achieved."

The platform came to a halt and Finn was ushered into another chamber. The light in this chamber was different than the others he had visited. It was filled with a soft golden light and a sound that Finn did not recognise, but which could be heard faintly and continuously. In front of him was what looked like a conveyor belt. It started to move and as it did, five opaque objects came into view.

"Those are seedpods," explained Karibar. "They house the elders when they are resting."

Karibar started to hum in tune with the sound which filled the chamber, and as he did, each seedpod became transparent. A white mist started to emanate from the top of each pod which materialised itself into the shape of a body.

"Elders do not have any physical form. They are beings of pure light. They take on the shape of the form in front of them so that they can communicate more effectively."

Finn was awestruck as the beings transformed into tall stately bodies which shimmered, sending shadows dancing across the walls of the chamber. He could not make out their facial features but he felt they were smiling at him and he felt totally at peace. Any worry he had ever had in his short life now seemed completely unimportant in the presence of these magnificent beings. He noticed his breathing had become deeper and slower than normal.

One of the beings came forward and Finn heard the words that were spoken to him in his head as clearly as if the being was speaking to him out loud.

"We welcome you, Finn. We have watched with interest your development and knew that your curiosity about life would eventually bring this moment to us all. You have attuned yourself to the natural rhythm of nature. This has served you well and allowed the communication with animals and birds that most humans have been unable to achieve. You will only lose this ability if you forget that you have it and do not continue to practice it. As you grow, your life will make many demands on you, as will the others who share it. My advice to you is to make time for yourself and continue to communicate with the universe as you do now through your daydreaming. In this way your questions will always be answered and a light will shine in the darkness to show you the way.

"Your role in life will become more apparent to you as you grow older, but know this: you have created a bridge of communication between worlds that has not existed for many generations. Your interest and love for the various life forms that you live beside has brought about this development. This bridge must not be destroyed. It will be instrumental in bringing much needed knowledge to your race in times of fear and desolation. At that time there will be those who think that their world has come to an end and there will be others who will celebrate in knowing that their new world has only just begun. I will say no more at this time but you will remember and act on my words instinctively. Go now in peace and with gratitude for all that you are and will become, for true success is a reflection of what you have become, not what you have achieved or accumulated."

The being stepped back and all five dissolved back into their seedpods. The conveyor belt started to move and the pods disappeared from sight.

Finn felt a deep humility he had never experienced before. He looked at Karibar who was smiling at him. Karibar put his hand on his shoulder and led Finn back onto the platform.

"There is one more sight we would like you to see before you leave."

He took Finn to one more chamber where an archway had been cut into the rock. Karibar motioned to Finn to walk through the opening. As Finn looked deep within the heart of the mountain he saw an immense fire with violet flames. They leapt up and filled every corner and crevice in the rock with warmth and light. Although the fire was the biggest he had ever seen, the heat and noise were not intrusive and Finn felt he could stare at it forever.

"This is the heart of the Gaia Spirit," explained Karibar. "This fire has the power to change dark into light, sorrow into laughter, and illness into health. Any being on any galactic system can use the power of this fire simply by calling upon it. It is this heart which our labours in this mountain and those of our brothers in New Zealand help to keep beating. Should this fire ever be extinguished, darkness would befall all who live here, and evolution on a physical level would no longer be possible. Only then would the warnings, often given of the end of the world, become a reality.

"Now, our journey has ended and it is time for us to rejoin the others."

They stepped back onto the platform and the ascent through the mountain began.

Chapter Twelve

A Fond Farewell

Finn was not aware of the journey back to the upper chambers. The noise that greeted him on his arrival soon brought him back to attention. The chamber had been filled with decorations and was packed with lively little men laughing and singing.

"This is a momentous occasion," said Geroma who was waiting for him as he stepped off the platform. "So, we decided to celebrate it in a way that I think we are all familiar with. We are having a party!"

Flutes, drums, and string instruments played and the men danced around each other drinking out of silver tankards. Karibar offered a tankard to Finn and encouraged him to drink. The liquid was warm and tasted quite sweet. Once inside, it warmed every part of his body and gave the same feeling of contentment that came from eating a hearty meal. Finn was approached by one of the men who invited him to join in the dancing. He recognised him as the man he had spoken to in the woods, only now his eyes sparkled, and a smile had replaced the scowl. Finn felt happy, very happy, and in no rush to leave the mountain or this strange race of people who lived here.

The party came to an end far too quickly and Geroma, accompanied by the same three men, escorted

Finn out of the mountain, through the woods, and back to his bedroom window. He had no idea what time it was or how long he had been away. The night was as black as when he had first set out and he had a feeling that very few minutes had actually passed. He waved to the men as they jumped over the wall and disappeared from view. Back in the familiar surroundings of his bedroom, he closed his eyes and remembered no more.

Chapter Thirteen

In the Cold Light of Day

Finn was awoken by the sunlight streaming though the gap in the bedroom curtains. A cool breeze blew through the window which was still slightly open. He lay for a minute, not sure whether his memory of the night before was going to be clear. It was, and he remembered every last detail of his trip inside the mountain. He felt his ribs and they no longer ached or were sore to touch. He felt full of energy and knew he must go to the woods and tell the badgers what had happened. He rushed down his breakfast, carried out his chores as quickly as he could, ran up the road and scrambled up through the bracken into Badgers Hollow.

He knocked gently on the bark of the tree where the badgers lived. He heard some scuffling noises and it was Arnold who pushed his nose out first.

"What's up, lad?" said Arnold sensing Finn's excitement.

"I've something to tell you both," said Finn.

The badgers settled themselves down on the leaves. "Well, go on then, dear," encouraged Amelia.

"The men who've been collecting the pebbles. I saw them, last night. They took me to the mountain and showed me around inside."

Arnold looked at him sternly. "Why didn't you come for us?"

"I couldn't. I looked for you both though."

"So, tell us, dear," asked Amelia in a reassuring voice. "Why are they taking our pebbles?"

Finn tried to explain to them that the men who visited the woods meant no harm, and none of the animals should be frightened or worried. He explained about the energiser and how the pebbles were needed to keep it going. Finn tried to describe the elders and how they looked after the work that went on in the mountain. He talked about the little men and the party they had after Finn had met the elders. Finn couldn't contain his excitement and, as much as he tried, the animals had taken some convincing, Finn was not all together sure he had been successful.

"Look," he said in frustration. "We'll go now and then you can see for yourselves."

116

The badgers nodded their heads in agreement and followed him. By the time they got to Mount Shallien, a trail of animals lined the route. They arrived at the base of the mountain and Finn scanned the rock face looking for the stone with the symbol on it. It was nowhere to be seen. He hit the rock with his hand, calling out both Karibar and Geroma's names. No response came from inside the mountain.

Frustrated and close to tears, Finn turned to face his audience. "I'm sorry," he whispered, "I really am, but I'm telling you the truth."

Arnold walked up to Finn and spoke softly to him.

"It's alright, son, we know that, we don't doubt you for a minute." Then he turned to the animals. "Come on everyone, let's leave the lad be. I think we can all go home now."

Finn couldn't hide his disappointment and sank to the ground and buried his head in his hands. For a brief moment he wondered whether the visit inside the mountain had been nothing but a vivid dream. That moment passed and he knew for certain that this was not the case. For now though, that didn't help to pacify his mood and in a sudden moment of realisation, he jumped up and ran through the woods.

Finn arrived at Tom's shack and banged on the door. It swung open of its own accord and Tom was sat in front of the fire smoking his pipe. Finn trembled as he stood in front of his friend. He gave the photograph to Tom. Tom stared at it before waving to Finn to sit down.

"Guess you're wondering who this is with yer pa hey?" asked Tom not taking his eyes off the picture.

Finn nodded even though he knew Tom wasn't looking at him.

"It's me," said Tom, finally looking up at Finn. He gave him back the photograph. "Yep, that's me. Yer pa was my brother, my younger brother by 'bout four years.

Me and him, we used to explore these woods together. Talked to badgers and other animals we did. It were our secret. We never told anyone, not even our parents knew 'bout it. Spent hours and days just roaming freely – like you do now."

Tom filled his pipe before continuing. "Well, see, I started down mine when I were fifteen year old. Sort of gave up on the woods. Had other things on me mind, like finding a wife. Yer pa went same way and soon he had met yer ma. Things just changed. I were working as the foreman and yer pa were on my team. I were right strict with all me men, including him. I knew he were ill but it didn't stop me docking his wages when he didn't come to work. Anyhow, there were a row 'bout shift hours and who were working what. I'd done shift rotas and I wasn't going to change them. The men wouldn't accept what I'd said and went to the management, but they didn't care and told men to get back to work.

"The men were right mad and called a strike. I kept going to work though, cos it were me who'd done rotas and if I went on strike too, it'd be like admitting I were wrong. I thought I were just doing me duty. Stupid and naive like, but I were too proud to see sense then. Every morning I walked through picket line. The other miners threw stuff and hollered names at me. Soon me missus couldn't even go out without the other women calling her names. In the end she wouldn't leave the house. Even folk I'd known all me life started to avoid me. Yer ma and pa stopped talking an' all. Said I'd brought disgrace on family and vowed never to speak to me or me misses again. When yer pa died, yer ma wouldn't have me near." Tom's voice was quiet and strained as he finished his sentence. "Lost me wife and son not long after yer pa died.

"Anyhow, when strike were over, the mine got rid of me and said I couldn't be trusted no-more. Truth is the men wouldn't work with me no longer so the mine sacked me to keep them happy. Made me realise what a bloody idiot I'd been, but by then it were too late. Yer pa was gone, so were my family and yer ma wouldn't look me in the face."

Tom picked up a pen knife and started to sharpen a pencil.

"I've always looked out for you lad, since you've been coming up here. You remind me of yer pa, in so many ways. I wish I'd done more for you though. I wish I'd done more for yer pa as well."

"I'll speak to ma," said Finn suddenly with a determined voice. "Look, you're the only family I have now 'part from her, and I aint going to let that mine ruin our lives – not anymore."

Tom's eyes followed Finn as he stood and ran out of the door.

Finn's vision was blurred with tears as he ran back home. His mother jumped, startled at his sudden appearance at the door. She stayed silent sensing his mood. Once again he took the photograph out of his pocket and let it fall onto her lap.

"Tom," stammered Finn. "That's Tom, my uncle and you knew all this time. You knew he were up in them woods on his own."

"You don't understand - you're just a child."

"So help me to understand – I want to understand."

Finn was aware that his voice was raised. He had never shouted at his mother before.

His mother took a deep breath and told a similar tale to the one he had heard Tom tell him not an hour before.

"Is that it?" asked Finn, when she had finished. "Does that mean that Tom has to be punished for the rest of his life? Is that what pa would have wanted?"

"I don't know how to make things right," whispered his mother. "Not anymore."

"Then I'll help you ma, we'll make it right together – you'll see."

No more words came from either of them. Finn stood in front of his mother, still shocked from the revelations he had heard. She lifted her head and looked up at her son's tearstained face. She stood to face him and held out her hand, motioning for Finn to take hold of it. Finn took a step forward, his mother reached out and held him tightly. It was as if he had opened a door, and all the grief and pain that had welled up inside of the pair of them had finally found a way out. As he held his mother's weight in his arms, he noticed how tiny and frail she had become. He closed his eyes and thought about the purple fire in the mountain and prayed as hard as he could that it would find a way into his mother's heart.

Chapter Fourteen

Thirteen Years Later

Thirteen years later Finn was walking his chocolate Labrador Suzie through Tyndale Wood. It had only been a few weeks since his last visit but his mother's health was deteriorating and she was not as mobile as she had been a year ago. The cottage was slowly falling into disrepair despite his constant attention. He knew it was only a matter of time before it would have to be sold and his mother moved into sheltered accommodation. Whatever the outcome, Finn was determined to continue to look after her welfare, as well as she had looked after his.

The village graveyard was also in a state of disrepair. It was lined with tombstones of men who had been still in their prime or barely into old age when they had sacrificed their lives working down the mine behind a mask of honour and tradition. Families without fathers and grandfathers had become more common, and as time passed, new people with cars who could travel easily had started to move into the village. Houses began to look cared for again. Finn couldn't help but feel that the change in the air was a much-needed relief from the shackles which had held this village captive for such a long time.

Finn walked along the worn path past Badgers Hollow and stopped. Suzie had caught the scent of another animal and pawed furiously at a hole by the base of a tree.

Finn stood and looked at the tree. He was sure it was the same tree he had leant against that Friday afternoon after school, despite all the bushes around it being overgrown. He remembered that eventful week when he first met the badgers, and the adventures that followed. After his visit inside the mountain, life in the wood had carried on as normal and sightings of the little men became less frequent. Eventually the excitement of what had happened slowly disappeared into the back of the minds of all concerned. Finn had continued to roam the woods and meet up with Arnold and Amelia until they eventually passed away. He missed his friends, but knew that their role had finished, and now future generations of badgers had taken their natural place in the woods.

Tom became a good friend as well as an uncle, and Finn spent many pleasant afternoons and evenings with him. In the summer, Tom would light a small fire outside the shack and cook the fish he had caught in the stream that day. In the winter a large black pot full of rabbit stew would bubble over a roaring fire inside the shack. He would listen intently as Finn chatted about his life in and out of school and about the goings on in the village. Finn had told Tom in great detail about his visit inside the mountain. He told him about Geroma and Karibar and the purple fire. Tom had listened silently, nodding occasionally as if to confirm what he was saying.

Finn's mother knew about the friendship that had developed between Tom and Finn and never complained. It was almost as if by giving her approval, she was somehow rebelling against the village and at last standing up for herself. She sent Finn with small food parcels and anything else she could afford, including the tools and clothes in the boxes from the shed. She had invited Tom to the house on a Sunday for dinner, but Tom had politely refused the invitation, preferring to stay out of sight and hopefully out of the minds of the villagers.

It was on the evening of his fifteenth birthday that Finn found Tom lying on his bed in the shack, his piercing blue eyes open, staring directly above. Finn had tried to wake him, thinking he had slipped and banged his head. The doctor at Helmsbury Hospital said he had had pneumonia and was lucky to have survived as long as he had done in the woods. Finn visited his grave every week and made sure the lilies, Tom's favourite flowers, were replaced.

The gypsies never returned to Tyndale and Finn never saw his friend again. He often wondered if Ryan was still travelling around the countryside and if their paths would ever cross in the future. Even if they didn't, he was grateful that he had known Ryan and that he had been a part of his life – no matter how briefly. Finn put his hand in his jacket pocket and pressed the small brass shamrock into his palm. He had decided that when he had children of his own, he would take them to the cave to look at the etchings he and Ryan had made on the wall, while the storm raged outside.

As Finn had grown older, his thirst for more knowledge drew him away from the village and into the city to attend university and study natural science. His Mother had been surprised and disappointed when he had announced his intention to go away to study. She had firmly believed that he would follow his father down the mine, as he had followed his father before him. She hadn't foreseen, as many others in the village hadn't, the mine's decline and subsequent unemployment that befell most of the communities around that area.

One by one the younger generation moved away to find work and make a new life. Few remained to take on the running of the shop or the inn. The blacksmith's son had chosen to go north to the Scottish borders where there was still a demand for his skill. When Christian's father lost his job in the mine, Christian also lost his position in the pecking order with the other children in the village. He seldom went out alone, and made no attempt to find alternative work when his dream of working down the mine was shattered. Occasionally he would walk to the local shop and purposely cross over to the other side of the road if he saw Finn coming towards him. His family had had to move out of the large house provided by the mine as it was to be sold off with all the other real estate. The council had built some new houses on the outskirts of the village to house the unemployed miners. It became known as 'the scheme' and the new people in the village often avoided going near it.

Mr Shuttleswaite retired as postmaster and community police officer and had not been replaced. Instead, a new police station was built in Helmsbury, and police cars patrolled the village, especially 'the scheme' throughout the day and night.

After the mine had closed, accusations were cast in several directions, and some residents stayed there in the belief that all would right itself and normal life as they saw it would be restored. Finn knew that would never happen and that he would never return to live in Tyndale. His path would continue to take him overseas to lands that needed further investigation.

After graduating from university, Finn had joined a team of scientists on an expedition to Antarctica. The ice shelves were melting faster than had previously been predicted and Finn was determined to gather enough evidence to present to a worldwide audience. As his career progressed, he became a well known and respected scientist, regularly filing reports for television and radio stations on environmental issues. Finn's unusual gift often enabled him to foresee and report the consequences that human behaviour would have on the earth, before it happened. He worked tirelessly in an attempt to educate people and encourage a deeper understanding of the planet and the universe.

Finn never forgot his visit inside Mount Shallien or the words that had been spoken to him by Geroma, Karibar and the elders. As his life unfolded, he had watched the world change and as these changes continued, he understood more fully what he had been told. Admittedly at times, he had struggled to keep up his connection with nature, but a silent promise that had been made many years ago rested inside his heart and would never be broken.

The End

About the Author

Julie Sandilands is originally from Cheshire where she lived until 1997. After completing her B.Ed. (Hons), in Business and Information Technology, she spent 3 years in Botswana teaching in a large government secondary school in the capital, Gaborone. She moved to Scotland in 2000 and now lives in rural Fife, Scotland with her son Duncan.